DHAMPIR'S WISH
Christmas Special
BLOOD LEGACY SERIES
ELISE HENNESSY

This novel is entirely a work of fiction. The names, characters and incidents portrayed in it are the work of the author's imagination. Any resemblance to actual persons, living or dead, events or localities is entirely coincidental.

Flutterbye Trail Press
797 Sam Bass Road #2541
Round Rock, TX 78681

First edition

Editing by Red Loop Editing
Cover Design by FrostAlexis Arts
E-book Chapter Art by Real Life Design
Published by Flutterbye Trail Press

ISBN: 978-1-954582-03-3 (E-book)
ISBN: 978-1-954582-05-7 (Print)

Feedback: Encounter a problem with this book? Let us know at elisehennessyauthor@gmail.com

Books by Elise Hennessy

Books in the Altare World

GRYPHON RIDER ACADEMY
Second Chance
Chosen
Storm Front
Wild Flight

ROYAL SPY INSTITUTE
The Crown Heist
Five & Chance

Also by Elise Hennessy

BLOOD LEGACY SERIES
Dream Walker
The Winter Key
Queen's Return
Court of Illusions
Shadow Dance
Rule the Night
Dhampir's Wish

Blood Curse
Blood Legacy: The Complete Series

Dhampir's Wish

Blood Legacy Series Christmas Special

Elise Hennessy

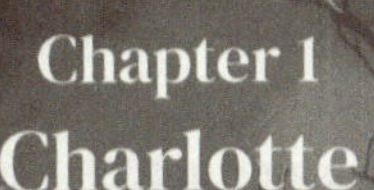

Chapter 1
Charlotte

CHARLOTTE CLICKED THE HEATER DOWN ONE NOTCH AND waited for her side of the car to cool. She was at the point where the heat was one click in between too toasty or weak enough to allow the chill of a New York winter deep into her bones.

"We done yet?" she grumbled to her partner, Armando Nizzola, who tapped the wheel to the rhythm of a sappy pop song playing over the radio.

He glanced to the analog clock on the dash, which clearly read 2:54 AM. "You tell me, *amica*," he answered with that rolling Italian accent of his.

Charlotte liked the way he spoke his vowels. And that, amongst other things, was how she knew she was falling for him. But it wasn't the quick, lightning-laced plummet of a lifemate's near-instant adoration for a perfect other half. Her attraction to him was an unplanned belly flop into a pristine pool. It made ripples. It had consequences.

Apparently, she was at the part of her patrol where she became a poet.

"I see it. One more hour," she sighed. The two of them were enforcers, a type of police for vampires. They sat watching a busy hub for supernatural activity, but unlike most nights, this one was whisper silent.

"Why so grumpy tonight?" He flashed one of his carefree, luminous smiles that did funny things to her insides. Despite being a Master vampire well into his two hundreds, he still bore a tan from his Mediterranean home to contrast his pearly whites perfectly.

"I've been stuck in this car with you for too long," she said.

He tisked. "Starting to sound like my uncle already. 'Can't wait to get a break from your voice,' he would say."

"Like he'd ever say that."

"He did! But we also never took breaks, so..." He shrugged with his palms up.

"You miss him?" she asked. His uncle Julian had finally retired from street duty. Despite being a ranking member in their coven and personal friends with the leader, he'd insisted on being on the front lines of various coven wars and conflicts. Now he was a combat instructor and enjoying the good life with Charlotte's best friend, Olivia.

"I miss not having his responsibilities," Armando said cheerfully.

"You don't like the sound of Head Enforcer Nizzola?" she teased, getting the same cringe from him that always accompanied the title, like it barely belonged to him. Most people never saw this reaction, the chin tuck and shoulder lift that made him look like a retreating turtle. But here in the middle of a light snowfall on their last patrol before the new year, he did the turtle tuck for her eyes alone. "Maybe you need conditioning. Should I just follow you around calling you that?"

"Please don't." He sounded embarrassed, but no blush followed. She'd never seen him blush.

Just vampire things, she thought. She could still blush under her dark complexion.

She blew out a sigh. "Truth is, I *am* grumpy tonight," she said, familiar frustration bubbling up in her chest. "I got a lead on my father."

Armando snapped upright. "You did?"

"Yeah..." She affected an uncaring shrug. "I've been looking for him again. Got a tip from one of my old Coven Rosas friends that they'd met a vamp named Darius down in Pittsburgh."

His smile was fading as he caught her tone. "Not the right one?"

"Nah. I got ahold of his social media. Definitely not the right guy."

"Sorry to hear that," he said, which she nodded to.

Silence hung between them.

Charlotte knew three things about her father: he was a vampire, his first name was Darius, and he had vitiligo. Such a distinctive combination of factors should've made him easier to find, yet she was nearing a hundred herself with nothing to show for her searches.

He's probably dead, she told herself. It happened a lot to vampires. The older ones picked each other off in the culminations of centuries-old plots or grudges that could span multiple immortals' existences...or just murdered each other out of sheer boredom. The death of a coven master in particular caused infighting and chaos that could make covens implode like a black hole. At any point, her father could've been a bystander of such pointless violence.

Despite that, she still searched. She still hoped.

"I just wish I could find him. That would be the perfect Christmas present," she said with a sigh.

Armando considered with a thoughtful tilt of his mouth before snapping his fingers. "Oh, what do you want for Christmas?"

She slanted an eyebrow. "It's in, like, four days."

"I still have four days to get you something, then!"

Typical Armando, she thought, fighting to keep a serious face. In truth, she hadn't gotten him a gift yet either. She'd been too busy listening to her two friends angst over what to buy their significantly older immortal mates, considering both men had everything they wanted already. Add in her search for her father, and it'd just slipped her mind.

"You know, whatever. Carve me something." Woodcraft was his hobby after all. "How about you? What do you want?" she asked.

His lips lifted. "Same. Whatever. Unless you have something cool and magical lying around?"

"If I had something fae made, I'd be keeping it," she said. So, they were in the same boat. Given that they weren't even a couple, she shouldn't have a drop in her chest from sudden anxiety, belatedly realizing she had the same problem as her friends. What could she buy Armando that he didn't already have?

"The boss is throwing a Christmas Eve party." Armando's voice drew her out of her thoughts. "Do you want to go with me?"

Her heart beat like a bird fluttering against its cage. "Like, as friends?"

From the look in his eyes, his thoughts may have slid along the same lines as hers. "It could be a date instead," he offered.

No, it really couldn't. She'd said it before, and she'd say it again if his expression didn't betray that he already understood nothing had changed yet. His chocolate brown eyes simmered to the brim with emotion. "I don't care what you are, *amica*. Give a man a chance," he murmured. "Dhampirs still live a *long* time."

"I'm just not ready yet." She repeated the same line she'd been saying for over a year. She couldn't go into a relationship with a vampire knowing that, as a dhampir, she was slowly aging. It'd taken a hundred years to look like she was in her youthful early thirties, where they matched in energy and appearance. The first hundred years for a half-vampire were the time when they could most easily pretend to be immortal. But add on another hundred years, and she'd be slowing down and visibly aging. A hundred more, and she'd be perpetually elderly until something finally took her down.

She'd decided ever since her actual twenties that she would avoid anything too complicated with a vampire. They lived too long and changed too little—could she really rely on one to take care of her when she entered the extended twilight of her life?

But that thought was cold and lonely when Armando was right there, sadness hunching his shoulders. She clicked the heater back up a notch. "I'm really trying to find him," she said to his profile.

Things would be so different if she found her father, the

source of the vampirism in her. He was the only person who could turn her fully. Her body simply wouldn't respond to anyone else attempting the ritual with her—and she'd tried.

Armando rested his forehead against the window. "I know it's a wild thought, but have you tried magic?"

"To find him?"

"Yeah. Or maybe something fancy to turn you without his blood," he said, a glimmer of an idea in his eyes.

"I was going to try the Dragon Lady soon," she admitted.

"She likes me more. Let me talk to her first."

"Fine."

"Fine," he echoed at a higher pitch, laughing when she swatted his shoulder. "Don't be jealous, I just have a way with ladies. Even five-thousand-year-old ones."

"I thought it was four thousand," she said.

"The age changes every time. I don't think she knows for sure." He shook his head at the thought. "Wouldn't that be something, though, if we found your father by Christmas?"

Her heart twisted wistfully. "It'd be a wish come true."

Chapter 2
Armando

ARMANDO WENT TO SEE THE DRAGON LADY WITH HIS HEART in his throat. He and Charlotte had started calling her thus when they'd realized the ancient fae had future sight and could divine every moment they called her by her real name, Izell Firebrand.

They gossiped about her *a lot*.

For all her status as the eldest fae alive and savior of the known supernatural world, to Armando and Charlotte, she put off the grumpiest vibes. It was part of the charm. Izell was still recovering from a difficult pregnancy, so their unit was often recalled for her every need. Their boss bent over backward to keep Izell happy.

"Armando, take me in your box to the book vendor," was her favorite request. He and Charlotte would wait in the car for her to buy armfuls of glossy paperbacks.

But that wasn't where it stopped. *"Armando, help me program this box,"* Izell asked of her phone.

"Armando, I need to visit the box store."

"Which one?" he would ask, because most stores were vaguely box shaped.

Izell would wave impatiently. *"The one that sells food in boxes. Why is everything in boxes on Earth? I swear mortals will evolve to have corners."*

He shook his head as he pulled up at her house on the

outskirts of town, alone. Charlotte's scent still lingered in the car, a festive cinnamon and pumpkin. A lot of girls walked around smelling like a pumpkin spice latte, but Charlotte could really pull it off. He was still catching his breath from their earlier conversation.

Charlotte had pushed him away from the d-word for over a year now. No dating; they were partners. She didn't date vampires. She was afraid of aging while her partner stayed the same. He tried to navigate around every excuse while accepting her boundaries. The lady didn't want to date, fine. But there was one small problem.

She was his lifemate.

He didn't mention it, because he knew she couldn't sense it. For a vampire, meeting a lifemate was about as subtle as a punch in the face. He'd known it the instant they'd met. She had to notice they had great chemistry, but for whatever reason, that wasn't enough. Keeping the lifemate connection to himself, he feared a new rebuff if he told that truth out loud.

He'd do anything in his power to help her out. Not only because she was supposed to be his one-and-done, his ride-or-die, but because she'd had a poor shake of life and deserved something nice. Dhampirs were easily controlled because, unlike their full-blooded brethren, they fed on blood once a month and felt a bond of loyalty to the donor. Charlotte had once become an indentured servant of sorts to a coven master who manipulated that bond to keep her close for decades. The only reason she'd escaped from the situation was the man having need of stronger bodyguards.

Charlotte fed from Armando now whenever the mood hit, and he let her do whatever she wanted. It was the right thing to do, the only way one should ever treat a dhampir. He wanted to put his fist through the throat of the coven master who'd treated her so poorly.

Still wearing a vicious grin at the thought, he got out of the warm car and hunched himself over on the walk up the drive. It was freshly cleared of snow, so he hoped Izell was in. Her house was as non-pointed as possible, custom built to be rounded with numerous circular windows. On experience, he knew the rooms were wedge-shaped.

If that didn't scream that an ancient, box-hating fae lived there, the yard was also filled with statues of various mythical beasties and snow-covered topiaries, which she'd successfully started shaping into more of the same before the first frost hit.

He wondered what Halloween was like in this neighborhood. Knowing Izell, she'd enchant her sculptures to groan and shift around in the spirit of the holidays.

The door opened on the third knock, and Izell's mate, Jaromir, answered. The man put a finger to his lips and let Armando in. Jaromir was one of the Blood Princes, an Ancient amongst vampires as one of the first.

His brown eyes twinkled, defining a long face and pale features. Everything he'd been through had aged him past the mid-thirties prime most of the Ancients appeared to be, giving him hints of gray in his blond hair and laugh lines around his smiling mouth.

To contrast, he wore shorts and a t-shirt printed with a sun shining over cheerful beachgoers playing volleyball.

Catching Armando's expression, Jaromir whispered, "It's a nice place, even at night."

"Isn't Corpus Christi in Texas?" Armando whispered back, reading the small print on the shirt.

Jaromir's lips pulled in amusement. "Texas has the best rocks, according to Izell."

Izell's voice called from another room, "You know I can hear you two, right?"

"Sorry," Jaromir called back. He didn't sound too apologetic and instead beckoned to Armando.

Courtesy of the circular house, there was a center room with angles like an octagon that usually served as the living room. The furniture and rugs were piled up around the edges, the bare wooden floorboards covered in glowing symbols and lit candles in a circle around Izell, who was sitting cross-legged in the center. The glow and flames all shone a golden yellow, the color of her magic.

Izell herself was a study in gold in her fae form, which she only glamored to cover up her nature amongst humans and the vampires who still didn't know fae existed. As an old astral fae, every inch of her skin was taken over by glimmering stars where she didn't wear the sandstone scales of her dragon. Since she was also a shifter, she had a dragon's whipcord tail wrapped around her lap and scales from the elbows down, with fingernails shaped like talons. Her eyes had no pupils, instead solid lenses of iridescent glitter set below an irritated scowl.

"Do you know what day it is?" she demanded.

"A, uh, bad day to bother you?" Armando ventured. He usually didn't walk into a spell like this, especially something so intricate.

"No, it's December twenty-first," she said, holding up a sharp claw. "As of midnight tonight."

He glanced to Jaromir, who was waiting with a patient expression. "December...oh," Armando said. "Midwinter."

"The longest night of the year. The best day for astral fae...*if* I can get some peace and quiet to make a connection to Faerie," she grumbled.

On cue, their baby started to cry in another room.

"I'll take care of her," Jaromir said immediately, striding away.

Armando stayed, clearing his throat. "Sorry to interrupt. I was just hoping you could help me with something," he said to Izell, who set her mouth in a stern line.

"What is it?" she asked.

"Can you help me find Charlotte's father? Like, with your magic?" He had his heart in his throat as she considered.

She glanced down at a rune on the floor, tracing the edge of its glowing surface. "I'm sure I *can*," she said. "But I require something in return."

Biting his tongue, he kept from answering. Bargains with fae, even innocent ones, always came with a price that needed to be fulfilled to the full extent of the wording. It was just how their magic worked.

She rattled off a vague address. "I need you to go into the

mauve box store and retrieve for me an extra-large Sophia in rose."

"Um..."

"Don't worry if they don't have that one specifically. Just bring me something from that store that fits me, and I'll consider your half of the bargain fulfilled," she interrupted with an impatient gesture. "Get Julian or something. He's good at tracking things down."

"That's people. He tracks people," he pointed out. But because she'd mentioned him, he'd still somehow rope his uncle along.

"Go get it, then. Don't come back until tomorrow," she said.

He saluted. "Yes, ma'am! One extra-large Sophia in rose from the...what kind of store?"

"Mauve box store," she repeated.

"But...what is *mauve*?"

"A color, you twit!"

Yeah, whatever. He'd figure it out. Hopefully.

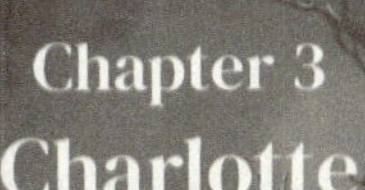

Chapter 3
Charlotte

SHE HEADED TOWARD IZELL'S CIRCULAR HOUSE SOMETIME before dawn, unconcerned that the sun may rise while she tried to speak to the Dragon Lady of her predicament. Charlotte had called in reinforcements in her two friends, Violet and Olivia. They'd all joined Coven Rehnquist at about the same time. While Charlotte was a thirty-something at heart, her two friends were literal thirty-somethings, young enough to be a rarity in vampire society.

Violet, a petite blonde, sat up front, fiddling with the clock-work gears of a fae-made magical tool called an occultarus. She'd decided to decorate hers like something out of a steampunk fantasy, with gears of variable sizes powering a set of copper butterfly wings that gave the shining orb the illusion that it flew on its own rather than by magic.

"Think she's in a good mood today?" she asked, her eyes flashing silver from a streetlamp. Violet was a Sorceress vampire, a rare cross between vampirism and fae blood that let her wield magic and use occultari. As powerful as that made her, one wouldn't know it when she'd bundled herself up in enough layers to resemble a marshmallow. Someone didn't do so well in the cold.

"Pfft. No," Charlotte laughed.

Olivia rested her head on the side of Violet's chair. "She'll change her mind the moment she sees us three good looking ladies at her door. It's hard to be mad when you look at us."

It was hard to even be annoyed with the woman in the backseat. She had a goofy, carefree grin, just a lady happy to be alive. Charlotte liked that vibe, even though she'd pulled her best friend's behind out of danger several times before Olivia had met and mated to a no-nonsense kind of man to take that job off her hands. Her mate Julian had learned to smile in the year they'd been together. And Olivia, well, she could be serious. Sometimes.

"Plus, if she *doesn't* help, then Violet and I have to figure out a tracking spell or potion. It's, like, her job to make sure we don't go off half-cocked," Olivia added.

"I don't think I agreed to that," Violet protested.

"Relax, Flowers, that's plan H. H for half—"

"Yeah, I get it." Violet blushed a steely color from her silvery-hued blood. Getting a nickname in their circle was a compliment; she just got flustered each time hers came up.

Charlotte parked the car, seeing tracks on the drive from another car that'd been there. It wouldn't surprise her if Armando had already come and gone, but she was going to try greasing the wheel too. If the sun came out while they spoke, Violet could make portals to take her and Olivia back to their respective homes, no harm done. While, as a dhampir, the sun didn't harm her. Small perks.

She went up to the porch, fist poised to knock. The hair on the back of her neck stood up, and a moment later, Violet cried out in alarm.

Charlotte jumped and shot a look over her shoulder to see Olivia holding a particularly ugly and misshapen statue with bat wings and a scorpion's tail at eye level. "I swear she gets new ones every time," she was saying.

The front door opened and Jaromir held a finger to his lips with a sigh as he leaned out of the threshold. "That's a manticore. And if you want to go inside, no loud noises," he whispered.

"Sorry," Violet said, her gloved hands in her puffy jacket's armpits as she shivered despite her layers.

"Jerry, is this enchanted?" Olivia asked, holding the statue by its tail as she inspected its underside.

Even a year ago, Charlotte would've had something to say about her calling a very ancient, very powerful vampire by anything but his actual name. But time had softened the guy, she thought. He seemed like a Jerry to her too.

"Yes, actually. Izell filled the tail with real manticore venom and sharpened the tail tip." He started to grin when she went still and eyed the spine a few inches from her arm. "I'd put that down before it senses you disturbed it."

Olivia went off to gingerly place it back on the ground, whispering profuse apologies. "It's not really enchanted," Jaromir confided while she was distracted.

"I figured," Charlotte murmured back.

Minutes later, the pressure in the air increased to a crescendo that left goosebumps all over Charlotte. She pulled her wool cap further over her ears. The feeling faded as Izell's voice hollered from inside the house. "Finally!"

The three women exchanged a glance. Jaromir stepped aside hastily. Izell's silhouette stood in the doorway, smoke billowing from her singed hair. Her glimmering eyes took them in as she grinned. "The way's open," she announced before pointing a hooked claw at Charlotte. "Why are you here?"

She opened her mouth to ask after her father, but Izell just kept talking. "Never mind, you're here for the same thing as Armando, right? I've been expecting you. Why don't you come with me?"

"Come with you?" Charlotte asked.

"Come with me to Faerie. You're all invited. It's midwinter! The longest night of the year." The fae seemed almost...giddy, bouncing on the balls of her feet as she spoke. "My people hold the Astral Light Festival all night to commemorate our victory over darkness when the new sun rises."

"It's fae Christmas," Jaromir whispered behind his hand. He was smiling over at Izell openly, catching her excitement and reflecting it in his own gentle way.

"Well..." This wasn't why they'd come to see her, and Charlotte couldn't think of how it'd help.

Olivia shuffled over to nudge Charlotte. "Are there things we could buy there?" she asked. "Like, fancy fae things?"

Charlotte held her breath, remembering that Armando had wanted something cool and enchanted. And neither of her friends were exactly satisfied with what they'd purchased for their mates.

Izell's eyes held a sly glint. "Of course," she said, gesturing the group inside. As Charlotte walked in last, the old fae grasped her shoulder. "As for your request..."

"My father?" she asked, earning a nod.

"There's a fortuneteller who always attends the festival. Rumor says she has the power to make real desires come true," Izell said.

She leaned in, immediately and intensely interested. If she required magical intervention to find her father and end the mystery of his disappearance, she'd take it. But there was an obvious "but" lurking in Izell's tone. "What's the catch?" she asked.

"Well, she requires you tell her one of your deepest secrets before sharing your fortune. That's the currency of the festival— secrets. Start thinking of what you're willing to tell, as true secrets are always more valuable than the secrets multiple people know."

Typical fae, Charlotte thought as she followed her inside and to a portal suspended in the middle of the house. The rip in reality pulsed with magic, currently clear and straight as a mirror, showing a snowy clearing on the other side. It was still nighttime over there, even though Faerie operated on different time than Earth.

They had a great view of a cluster of pines strung with multicolor lights. An adult fae ran by the portal's view, chased by a group of wingless fae kids obviously giggling as they lobbed snowballs at him.

"Looks like a great time!" Olivia announced, but her gaze was on Izell instead of heading through immediately.

"We should have a few hours there. The bridge between

Earth and Faerie collapses when Faerie's sun rises, so don't get too lost," Izell said with a dismissive wave. "This is a Seelie festival; you should be fine. Go have fun."

Olivia didn't need any more encouragement, heading through with an eager smile. "Should be?" Violet said, watching her go.

"Should be," the fae repeated. She strode away from her own portal, returning with her swaddled baby. Charlotte smiled as she caught a glimpse of baby Gwyneth Anderon's face. She felt a little kinship for the half-fae child, who looked so human save for the sparkles in her baby blue eyes and the fine points of her ears.

Izell was in a hurry to leave, grasping Jaromir's hand and plunging into the portal next.

Charlotte pushed Violet through when she hesitated. "C'mon, Flowers, live a little," she teased a split second later. Traveling through a portal was a quick plunge into cold darkness. Charlotte always shut her eyes tightly when using one, else she'd have a belly full of nausea from the sudden shift in air pressure and location between one step and the next.

Faerie was said to be a place of great beauty, but she was still stunned as she took in the view. It was like she'd walked into a perfectly saturated photo of a snowy wood, except every pine and bush was lined with lanterns and multicolored floating orbs of light. A velvety curtain of darkness lay overhead, full of crushed diamond stars.

She spotted streamers and brightly painted tents through the woods, where the sound of live music drifted from, punctuated by the happy cries of children. What'd caught her attention the most was the scent of warm nutmeg and cinnamon, hopefully from baked goods. Her belly rumbled quietly at the thought.

Her friends were already headed toward the festival, so she took a moment to crouch down and form two snowballs.

"Hey, Olive!" she called. Olivia turned, wearing a smile of wonder. Charlotte pelted her across the face with perfect aim, one snowball after another.

"Oh, it is *on!*"

They traded volleys of snow as Violet watched, holding her occultarus and standing out of range. Any errant snowballs that went her way melted from a shield of warm air she'd cast around herself. Charlotte focused on assailing the other woman instead, giggling like a schoolgirl as her stress melted away for a few blissful minutes.

She even laughed when the snow around her leapt up and heaped upon her and Olivia in a mini avalanche. Violet's hand was still glowing as she said, "I win!" Booking it toward the festival, the Sorceress laughed as she dodged a salvo of snowballs.

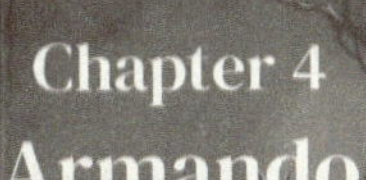

Chapter 4
Armando

"Run it by me again. What are we looking for?" Julian Fairfax asked from the driver's side as they cruised downtown.

It was weird to have him driving. That was always Armando's role when they were patrolling partners. But now his eyes were peeled as he looked for... "A mauve-colored store," he said, pointing out one boutique amongst many. "Does that look mauve to you?"

Julian slowed the vehicle, and they stared at the building's façade intently. It didn't help that the location Izell had shared encompassed several blocks of specialized boutiques and quirky stores.

"It could be," he said after a pause. "Eventually, you'll just have to go into a store and try your luck."

They both looked down at Armando's phone, where he'd pulled up an Internet search of "mauve" just to find that it included several shades somewhere in the range of pink, purple, or gray.

"She's a woman; she'd want you to go to a pink store," Julian said.

"You sure, though? It's Izell. She's more of a gray kind of lady to me."

"Or she'd want you to go to the opposite of what you're thinking." They shared a bemused glance.

Armando sighed. "Let's do another loop. Maybe we missed something obvious." He had another reason for the suggestion. It looked like his uncle was chewing on a thought. Julian was one to overthink, so Armando waited, mostly patient, for what was bothering him. Considering he'd dragged Julian from his home right after nightfall, it was big, whatever it was.

He took another sip of coffee as he scanned the buildings. They blurred together, part of the cityscape he'd seen thousands of times. He knew he should've asked Izell for more details. But it wasn't completely her fault—he had barely slept with a head full of warring anxiety and excitement.

"So, what did you get Olivia for Christmas, man?" he asked when he couldn't stand the silence between them any longer.

"A ring."

"Oh, neat, going for some shine, hmm? Chicks dig a little flash," he said, flipping his hand.

"An *engagement* ring," Julian clarified with a sigh.

His tension suddenly made complete sense. Julian was about as tight as a bowstring, so it was good to get him away from the missus for a bit. Olivia had an uncanny ability to read body language and tone, and if she'd been around him like this, she'd know something was up within a heartbeat.

Armando propped his chin on a fist. "So, you're nervous about a human ritual? You two are already mates and all."

"You don't understand. I'm proposing at the party in a couple days." Julian rubbed his temple.

"In front of the whole coven," Armando said with a gasp. "The boss didn't even do that!"

Their coven master, Alexander Rehnquist, had snuck away with Violet to return to the island nation where they'd become mates to propose to her privately. Beforehand, if Armando was a betting man, he'd have put money on Julian opting for privacy and Alex opting for something flashy and opulent.

"Olivia will like it more." Julian spoke with certainty.

He snapped his fingers. "Ah! I get you. But how are you going to keep it a secret when you're a nervous wreck?"

"Olivia's out with the girls tonight. I have time to get it together." He scrubbed his face as they stopped for a red light. "You see your shop, by the way?"

"Uh..." Armando had gotten distracted again.

"We're stopping at the next pink store," Julian said. He did just as he'd suggested, gesturing for Armando to get out of the car. "I'll circle around."

"Thanks, man." Armando looked up at the boutique's name, which seemed French and was written out in fancy script. Its storefront was a nice pinkish-purple, the paint bright and fresh for the Christmas shopping season.

He hoped he wasn't about to embarrass himself by walking in and asking the store for something it didn't carry. What was an "extra-large Sophia in rose" anyway?

As he hesitated outside, a pair of mortal women left the store and descended the stairs to the sidewalk. One caught his eye and batted her lashes over the rim of her glasses. Out of habit, he flashed a smile just wide enough not to show fangs as he stepped out of their way.

"Hey there. Want to see—?"

He was trotting up the stairs before she could finish her sentence, dodging a situation he would've embraced only a year ago. He used to flirt with anyone with a pulse, but now, the thought turned his stomach.

The door slammed behind him with his haste to get inside, jangling a pair of bells on the handle.

He looked up and made eye contact with a startled gathering of women. Panning over their heads, he realized just what this store sold.

Lingerie.

It was a common misconception that vampires couldn't blush, but Armando was testament of the opposite. He felt his face flush with heat as he froze in mortification.

"Can I help you, sir?" asked an obvious employee as she sashayed over to him. Her uncomfortable-looking high heels punctuated each step with authority.

On the inside, he cursed Izell, because he knew this had to be the right store. He cleared his throat. "Do you have...an extra-large Sophia in rose?" He made sure to put as much cluelessness in the question as possible. It wasn't hard. He was already drawing in his shoulders and ducking his head. Charlotte told him the gesture made him look like a turtle. "It's...it's for my girl-friend," he added.

Thankfully, she seemed to have pity on him and went to check the store while he waited in the entryway. His embarrassment faded as he took in the establishment, which had a few fine pieces on display and plenty of bored employees milling around, waiting to give one-on-one attention to late holiday shoppers.

They were out of the particular piece Izell had requested. So, he ended up touring what was there anyway and grabbed some-thing at random that would fit her. He winced at the bill and left in a hurry, still feeling hot in the face when Julian stopped at the curb to pick him up.

"I think this thing is made of pure gold. It cost that much," he confided, showing off its silky hem as Julian pulled into traffic to take him directly to Izell to deliver it.

Julian's brows rose. "Hope it's worth it."

"Man, I'd buy her a mountain of...scanty clothes I don't want to imagine her wearing...if it means Charlotte finds her father," he said.

"You still haven't told her?" Julian asked.

"About what—the lifemate thing?" When he nodded, Armando blew out a sigh. "I haven't told her. She'll barely look at me if I try to flirt. I don't want to see her reaction to anything more when she's so preoccupied that she's aging and I'm not."

Julian grunted, letting the sound of slush under the tires be the only noise between them.

Armando just hoped this worked and that he could fulfill Charlotte's Christmas wish. It would be perfect—she could become a vampire at last and realize just how much restraint and patience he'd shown despite being known for having little of either. She was worth it, and waiting had taught him more about those values than hundreds of years of existence.

He realized Julian was watching him out of the corner of his eye. A knowing little smile tugged at his uncle's lips. "What?" he asked with a nervous chuckle.

"I'm proud of you," Julian said. "I hope Charlotte sees how lucky she is soon."

Armando felt his expression light up. It felt like his tough old pa giving him a gruff "good job" at the end of a long day of training. How times changed, to see Julian smiling and sharing in a different kind of hard work.

"Yeah, me too. Hopefully it'll be really soon," he said, wanting to frame this moment forever.

Chapter 5
Charlotte

By the time they made it to the festival, covered in snow, Izell and Jaromir were long gone. Charlotte figured that gave them free reign to explore with their wits about them. The festival itself was packed with various kinds of fae and their mythical friends straight out of a fairy tale. A unicorn with a prismatic horn and fur as pure as fresh snow meandered by, carrying three lesser fae children who could be flower-like triplets with their soft pink skin and orange hair.

Olivia clasped her hands as the unicorn passed them, the awe back in her expression. "Do you think the rumors about them and virgins are true?" she whispered to Charlotte.

"Probably. I think our days of riding sparkle horses have passed," she said with a dramatic sigh. Olivia echoed it, putting a wrist to her forehead in regret.

The festival looked like a pop-up market, with tents and attractions all over. She barely knew where to start. Except there was a signpost, which she scratched her head over. It was straight out of a children's storybook, with erratic arrows pointing every which-way, some with loops and double ends.

"Why don't we just wander?" she suggested.

She kept her eyes peeled for any sign of an obvious fortuneteller since "fortuneteller" on the sign had been one of the more convoluted arrows. They first found an astral fae wearing several strings of glowing beads like he was straight from Mardi Gras standing behind a booth with steaming hand pies and mugs of hot chocolate.

"Pies for a fib, mugs for a kiss," he said with a wink.

"Seelie fae can't lie, though," Charlotte pointed out, coming over when Violet stopped to waft the warm scent of pie toward her.

The dark fae's teeth sparkled like the stars that glimmered in his skin. "Can't we? We don't get humans in these parts often. First time?"

"Nah." If he wanted a lie, he got one. And he seemed to know it, as he handed her a pie in a thin paper wrapper. She passed it to Violet when she noticed the other woman eyeing it.

"What do you want for some beads?" Olivia asked.

He grabbed a fistful of strands, glancing down at them with a shrug. "One of your earliest memories. So far back it's nearly a secret."

Olivia considered for half a second. She told the story of her first dance class, frilly pink tutu and all.

They walked further in as she held up her new strand of beads, long enough to loop around her neck. "I think there's some sort of potion in these," she said thoughtfully, giving it a shake.

"Maybe they'll keep glowing, then," Charlotte said, slowing with an appreciative whistle a few tents in. She recognized a glowing occultarus, but most of the items for sale were odd and flashy implements that seemed related to casting magic.

The occultarus belonged to a fae woman who had a burgundy shawl pulled tight over her form. "Move along, ye with no magic," she said as Charlotte stopped to inspect the wares.

The fae turned her face away, but not before Charlotte caught a glimpse of her lavender-hued skin. She'd learned that unnatural shades usually marked an Unseelie. The line between the two sides of fae natures had blurred recently with the lifting of the Unseelie curse, so Charlotte wasn't sure if it would be truth or lies leaving the fae's mouth.

"I'm looking for something mostly harmless for a gift," she

said, her hand hovering over a painted skull that was about the size of her palm.

Her fingers closed around something else as the fae pushed it into her grasp. She inspected what looked like a wooden butter knife.

"Ye may desire that," the fae said, keeping her head bowed to avoid eye contact. "For the woodcarver in yer life."

Charlotte's gaze narrowed. How had this fae known about Armando's hobby?

"What does it do?" she asked.

"Whisper a true secret in my ear and maybe I tell ye."

She wet her lips, drawing on the short list of secrets she was willing to share with these stranger fae. While she supposed it was good fun for a race of tricky melee-mouths who probably convinced each other complete fabrications were their secrets, she didn't feel like lying and getting kicked out before visiting the fortuneteller.

Bending, she whispered over the woman's shawl, "I've spent a thousand hours plus on my favorite video game. But when my friend wanted to get into it, I pretend to be new so I could show off." She glanced over her shoulder to be sure Olivia hadn't heard her. She and Violet were busy watching a herd of satyr and faun perform an acrobatic routine.

"Hmph. Humans and their toys," the fae woman snorted. "The knife looks unsuited to the task but reads the intentions of the whittler. No mistakes will it make."

"Really?" She imagined it would be quite useful.

"Ye can take it for one more secret. Did yer friend ever notice yer deception?"

Charlotte smiled proudly. "No. I kicked her ass for weeks until she got better at it."

"Yer secret is safe with me. Now go, I have nothing else for ye." She waved her off with a smile in her tone.

Charlotte rejoined her friends, and they wandered further into the festival. It was bright as daytime around them from the lanterns hanging from the trees and booths. While Olivia and

Violet flitted over different offerings, from food to flowers to crafts, Charlotte stayed back and kept her ears open.

Now that she had something for Armando, she needed to find that fortuneteller before the night ended. She heard a few fae mention their fortunes. Most had painted runes on their hands and were studying them intently.

Charlotte wondered if this was the fae equivalent to a human fortuneteller. Someone who put on a good show but was ultimately a fake. That kind of performer was fun, but she wanted magic. She wanted it to be real.

Olivia's raised voice interrupted her thoughts. "Look, I gave you my best secret. I need more than this!" She flapped around what looked like a leather glove.

"It's a good deal, human," the fae man across the booth told her. "You don't even have the currency to afford it normally."

Charlotte came to Olivia's side and crossed her arms. "But what can she do with *one* glove?" She asked.

"Give it as a gift and see." He shrugged. "Or another secret and I'll tell you what it does."

Olivia ground her teeth as she and Charlotte exchanged a glance. "I'll give you a little one," Charlotte offered when she saw the crease of stubbornness between her friend's brow.

She had the fae man lean in and whispered in his ear, "I played the trumpet when I was in school." She wasn't kidding when she said it was small, but the honking and tooting she remembered from that time was best left forgotten.

He tapped on her shoulder and beckoned she turn her head. "One glove is all it takes," he murmured. "It's enchanted."

"What does that mean?" She asked.

"You'll see."

"So, she doesn't need to buy another glove or something?" Her brow raised. That didn't seem right.

He shrugged. "You can trust a Seelie."

Ah, now she was familiar with that phrase. She added how Izell ended it. "Except when you can't."

He crossed his arms. "Unlike you, I cannot lie. I stand by my word." And actually, she believed that. Somehow, one glove was enough. They were in Faerie; anything goes here.

She tugged Olivia away and shared his secret while the curly-haired woman put it away in a plain wooden box. A disbelieving frown was shot at her. "One glove, though? I wanted a whole getup. Oh well, I guess I'll just have to tell Julian one of my best secrets was only worth this much."

"Just add it to the mountain of gifts you're giving him anyway," Charlotte said with a laugh. Olivia and Violet had gone separate ways with their conundrum of what to buy. Olivia had at least six things she'd custom ordered while Violet had one big one. They'd spent about the same amount of money for different results.

"I could just give him a piece at a time. One for his birthday... if he remembers when that is..." she mused.

"I'm sure by the end, he'll be dying to know what you got him," Charlotte teased, earning a playful shove.

"Hey Char?"

"Yeah-huh?"

"Where's Violet?"

They both stopped and took a look around. Amidst the crowd of colorful fae, there was little sign of the petite blonde.

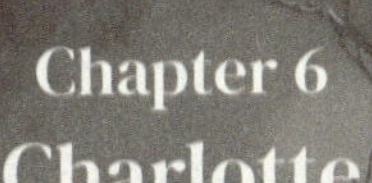

Chapter 6
Charlotte

"Okay, don't panic. This place isn't that big," Olivia said, taking deep breaths.

"She was just here." Charlotte wasn't too worried, at least not yet.

They decided not to split up, instead combing the immediate area for Violet. Finding a human at a fae festival should be an easy task. She could admit that they were dull compared to beings who wore stars, flowers, fire, or even clouds as if they were accessories.

Charlotte was about to call out to her using telepathy, yet another vampiric ability that was difficult for her to use consistently, when she blundered into a cloud of mini-fae. Flying around as a unit, they were tiny and glowing like lightbulbs with wings. She could make out the silhouettes of men and women within their light, pointed ears and little flowers and leaves worn like clothing.

"Oh, 'scuse me," she said. They alighted on her like a flock of roosting birds, resting featherlight atop her head and arms.

One of them waved into her line of sight upside-down, dimming its glow until she could make out a smiling face and pointed little nose. "Hi!" it exclaimed.

"You're a human!" another said.

The rest chattered in a chorus of squeaky voices. Charlotte

glanced to Olivia to share some disbelief, just to find her friend chasing one of the tiny creatures in circles while it giggled glee-fully. She scrubbed her cheeks instead. "Hello, yes, I'm...sort of human," she said. Half-human, close enough. "What are you guys?"

"Oh, a new person! We're pixies," the one hanging off her brow said.

"Right on," she said, distracted. "Have you seen another human?" A dozen little arms pointed toward Olivia. "Not that one. A third one?"

The pixies quizzed her on what Violet looked like before flut-tering off in all directions in search of her. Only the one clinging to her face remained. At least it transferred to her hand when she offered her palm, which allowed her to study it more closely. It actually seemed male to her, with gangly limbs and a shock of evergreen hair.

"Can you tell me where the fortuneteller is, too?" she asked.

"She's in the last tent!" He pointed the way they'd been going, with the flow of the crowd. "Did you want to make a wish?"

She nodded, watching a pixie approach and alight on her wrist. "Who were we looking for again?" the newcomer asked.

"I forgot," the pixie sitting on her palm admitted.

"You forgot already?" She wanted to bury her face in her palm.

More pixies drifted back to them, similarly unsuccessful, until one came and tugged on her jacket, fluttering off with a giggle. "C'mon, Olive," she said, catching her friend's shoulder and tugging her along to rush after the little ball of light.

Olivia took that moment to steal a pixie off Charlotte. "You're my Tinkerbell now," she informed it.

"Huh?" it asked. This one stayed on her shoulder at least.

They went around a few bends in the path about as compli-cated as the topsy-turvy signposts here and there amongst the festival. Violet stood in front of a vendor, holding a glass bottle full of chalky blue liquid. She flinched as Olivia called to her, "Hey! Are you really buying a *potion*?"

"Oh, hey guys." Violet put it down and flashed a grimace. "I must've drifted off, huh."

"It's not like we worried you'd been kidnapped by a fae or something." Olivia rolled her eyes. "But I got Tink out of the deal, so it's good. What potion were you buying there? I could fix you up, you know."

"I was just shopping. I'll just come back to this later." Violet glanced to the fae she'd been haggling with, who shrugged.

They stood in a gaggle, with more pixies landing on them for a rest. "Maybe we should visit the fortuneteller," Charlotte suggested. Even though she thought the itty-bitty pixie committee could also get them completely lost if they really had a gnat's memory.

The pixies asked dozens of questions as they went looking for that tent. "I'm not making a wish," Violet told one on her shoulder. "Maybe it'll give Charlotte's a better chance of coming true. Like less competition."

Charlotte ignored the chatter when she realized they were coming to the end of the festival and joining a line of fae waiting for their turn to talk to the mysterious fortuneteller. The clearing stopped behind the tent, ringing it with lanterns in a clear barrier. She watched the sky, hoping the stars would continue shining despite however long they had to wait.

"Izell mentioned the fortuneteller can make one wish come true. She must've heard so many by now," she said quietly.

"Yeah, but how many people made a wish with more than one person's secrets?" Olivia asked, looking thoughtful. "I saved a juicy one for her."

She blinked in surprise. "You did?"

"Of course! C'mon, you deserve something nice." She leaned over and whispered with a hand over the side of her mouth. "Besides, you and Armando are *so* cute together."

Warmth licked at her cheeks. "Are we?"

"Uh huh. And if you ask me, you've been a couple for a long time without actually making it official," she said.

If she were honest with herself, that was probably true. She just lifted a shoulder. "I can't lock him into a relationship unless this works." So, she dearly hoped the fortuneteller would listen to her wish above all the others whispered in her ear this night.

Her first glimpse of the fortuneteller didn't do much for her confidence. The woman was an average fae, skin brown like the earth. She wore robes, and a turban covered her candy pink locks except for a braid down her back. Numerous bangles coated each arm, clinking as she gestured, and two sets of hoop earrings quivered by her cheeks, each nearly wide enough to double as additional bracelets.

The woman was seated cross-legged on a cushion and beckoned for the fae in front of Charlotte to come sit down. They murmured together as the fortuneteller skimmed her finger over the other fae's palm. She reached to her side to draw a fine-tipped brush from a pot of paint. The tension in Charlotte's back knotted up as she realized she would soon be next.

She met the gaze of the fortuneteller, whose eyes were pure green with a hint of sparkle at the corners. Despite having no visible cornea, it still felt like she gave Charlotte a quick appraisal before beckoning her over.

"Good evening to you." She held her arm up to Charlotte's with a playful smile. "Seems we match. You are here to make a wish?"

"Yes. Do you want my secret first, or...?" The fortuneteller had already taken her hand and was reading her palm with a thoughtful frown.

"Hmm. How unusual," the fae murmured. "Will you come into the tent with me? I need to consult a book on human and vampire fortunes. Perhaps your friends can join us?" Her head tilted toward where Olivia waited with her hands clasped while Violet rubbed her shoulder and whispered in a soothing undertone.

They followed as the fortuneteller put up a sign and led them into her tent, which was pitched wide enough to contain a table and bookshelf comfortably. Charlotte stopped short when she saw Izell at the table with her legs up, drinking casually from a mug of tea. She held her daughter casually in the crook of her arm.

"Took you long enough to get here," she remarked. "Lovely tea tonight, Saniya." The other fae came over and took the baby to cradle.

"Hello baby Andie," the fortuneteller cooed to the child. "Did you cast the—?"

Izell cut her off with a flippant wave. "Yes, yes. No one will be able to hear or sense what's about to happen." She turned to Charlotte. "You might want to be sitting down for this."

She sat obediently, her brow creased in confusion until the moment Saniya took off her turban and exhaled. The fae's form blurred before her eyes, going from a pretty, pink-haired woman to something completely different. From the torso up, she was still feminine, but the waist down turned into a drifting column of smoke that hovered a foot off the ground.

Saniya's robes billowed at the bottom to their own personal wind. Suddenly, the turban would've made her look the part of what she was, matching every stereotype of a genie Charlotte could pinpoint. Her skin had shaded to scarlet, boldly complimented by her bangles and slitted eyes that glowed from within. They seemed to pierce right through to Charlotte's soul.

"My friend Izell said you had a wish for me," she said, her voice echoing with power.

Charlotte's mouth was dry with shock. "Uh...yeah," she managed. "Are you...really...?"

A smile revealed a hint of pointed teeth. "I'm a very well-kept myth. Just seeing me adds you to a spell of secrecy I maintain on myself. I'm Saniya, the last free wish-maker djinni."

She remembered her manners and led introductions for herself and her two friends. The djinni greeted them warmly before saying, "I can sense you all carry a deep desire in your hearts. Though my magic only allows me to grant one wish a day, perhaps you can still share what you want more than anything?"

Neither of them had said anything about a "deep desire," but Charlotte realized that was because of her. She figured they must've put aside what they wanted to help her, even to the point of not making a wish to give her a better chance. Well, here was a more direct chance, and she found herself getting emotional.

"You guys go first," she murmured so they wouldn't hear how she was choked up.

Violet and Olivia exchanged a glance, gesturing to each other to take the lead. Finally, Olivia spoke up. "There's only one thing I would make a wish on. I keep wondering... I'm an Alchemyst just like Queen Nyah. I can make potions and sense emotions like her. Does that mean I'm also a nephilim? Both the nephilim I know faced down a demon directly, and I...well, I had a chance, and I wimped out."

"I don't think anyone would call your situation wimping out," Charlotte said in surprise.

Olivia shrugged, a troubled frown tugging at her lips. "I also didn't fight a demon, which seems like the trigger."

Violet held up a finger. "Technically, we found that the trigger was exposure to demonic magic." She glanced over at her, rubbing her lips together. "I guess now that Jazrach's gone, it doesn't matter."

"That's right, it doesn't matter. I just wonder, you know?" Olivia shrugged.

The djinni nodded, her expression inscrutable as she turned to Violet. "What is your desire?"

Her mouth was half-open, hand resting on Olivia's in sympathy. "Um." Violet blinked rapidly, a silvery blush rising to her cheeks. "It's a little personal."

"I cannot help unless your wish is spoken aloud."

"Well, my fiancé is an older vampire, right?" She shifted in her chair under everyone's attention. "The older a vamp gets, the less fertile they are. And I want a baby."

Charlotte nodded in approval. Olivia released something between a cry and squeal, jumping out of her chair to hug Violet's side. "You want a family! Two-point-five little vamplings! Can I be auntie?"

"Definitely," Violet said, her blush fading as she released a laugh that visibly relieved the tension from her shoulders.

Saniya wet her lips, turning to Charlotte. It looked like she was trying not to smile. "And your wish?"

Moment of truth, she thought. "I'm looking for my father, a vampire," she said. "I've looked for him for a long time."

"Why is it so urgent now?" The djinni was definitely staring right through her with those glowing eyes.

"I want to be the real deal for a man. An immortal man." She thought of Armando's megawatt smile and couldn't help a wistful twist of her own lips. "But I can't entertain that idea if our theoretical life ends with me getting old and dying."

Saniya hummed. "It is the natural order of things, to love and grow old. But I see. I have good news for you all." She spread her palms with magic shimmering on her fingertips.

"She's still granting one wish, but..." Izell pointed to Violet. "We have remedies for your mate."

"And...little known fact to mortals." Saniya offered her glowing fingers to Olivia. "Djinn are demons."

"You are?" Olivia's face creased with sudden wariness.

Izell snorted, an eye roll in her tone. "She wouldn't be free right now if she hadn't earned it."

"I don't intend to fight you, but perhaps the touch of my magic will be *illuminating*." Violet caught the pun from Saniya and giggled heartily.

Olivia shook her head, taking the djinni's hand after a moment of hesitation. "I'm not even sure if I would know what to do with light magic," she said. "Just, you know, it'd be nice to have some closure. That it's the nephilim angel stuff that makes my blood gold instead of silver."

"Does this answer your questions?" As Saniya pulled away, cradled in Olivia's palm was a tiny ball of light. Considering how violent the awakening of a nephilim's power could be, Charlotte's awe was tempered with gratitude that Olivia didn't explode with it and potentially harm someone.

Olivia bounced to her feet and danced in place while cradling that bit of magic. "It's true! It's in my blood!" She drew herself up and intoned self-importantly, "It's my *legacy*."

Laughing in amusement, Saniya turned to Charlotte. "That leaves us with you. Are you ready?"

Charlotte quivered with anticipation as she nodded. "Don't

mind my third eye. It's just a djinni thing," Saniya said. "Stand and repeat your wish for me."

She got to her feet and cleared her throat. "I wish to be reunited with my father." Her heart leapt to her throat as the third eye made an appearance, opening vertically between Saniya's brows. Tingles ran their way over her skin as it felt like invisible magic caressed her.

The moment couldn't have lasted longer than a breath. The creepy eye closed, returning Saniya's features to normal as she smiled and clapped her hands. "Granted. Now, you all should be going before you are trapped in Faerie at dawn."

Charlotte made sure to hug the djinni first. While she seemed ethereal floating there, she was solid and strong as they embraced. "Best wishes to you. And Merry Christmas," Saniya whispered in her ear.

Chapter 7
Armando

Julian drove him to Izell's house, parking alongside a familiar car. "So this is where ladies night went," Julian commented as he cut the engine.

Armando gathered up the garment bag holding the lacy thing he'd bought Izell, hoping it was good enough. Because he'd probably die of mortification if he had to go back and get it exchanged.

"Kind of suspect, huh?" Armando commented. "That they came here. When I'm doing something for Izell and all."

His uncle shrugged. "We're all working toward the same thing. Also, speak of the Devil."

They watched the rosy-cheeked trio of Charlotte, Olivia, and Violet giggle their way to their ride. He was stunned anew to see Charlotte looking tired but carrying an air of happiness she hadn't had in a long time. She stopped short when they made eye contact through the thin barrier of the car's window.

He scrambled to get out and talk to them. "What are you doing here?" he and Charlotte asked at the same time.

"Jinx," she said quickly.

"Visiting Izell—aw darn it. What do I owe you for a jinx?"

She smiled wider. "Just give me a hug. It's nice to see someone normal."

"Implying Armando's normal," Julian said, gazing soulfully into Olivia's eyes as they clasped hands. Seeing that, Armando realized that it was past time for them to get engaged. He couldn't help a thrill of excitement that it'd be happening so soon.

"He's more normal than all the fae we just saw," Violet said, standing back and watching while Armando and Charlotte shared a hug. She clutched a little wooden box to her chest and shivered from a cold breeze. "It's midwinter! Fae Christmas!"

"It was great, but we've been up really late," Charlotte sighed.

"So, you're heading home? Without telling me how you were invited to fae Christmas and I wasn't?" Armando put a hand to his chest in faux hurt.

She patted his cheek. "Yup. See you later."

"Wait. At least tell me what it was like?" He didn't want her to go so soon. Her cheer was infectious, drawing him closer. Surely something amazing had just happened to get Charlotte in such high spirits.

"I will. But we just spent, like, an entire day in Faerie. I'm gonna saw some logs and then you'll hear all about it," she promised. "And you need to talk to Izell!"

"I do?"

"Definitely." Even Violet and Olivia were nodding, though the latter was still pressed close to Julian.

Armando had this feeling he was on his own again, confirmed when Julian tossed him the keys to the car. "I'm driving back with them. Good luck," his uncle said before opening the door for Olivia.

"Yeah, man, thanks," he sighed. He went to knock on the door, his knuckles striking bare air as Izell opened it a split second too early.

The fae's trademark scowl was absent. She waved him inside. "I have good news, and you have perfect timing."

He thrust forward the garment bag. "I got your thing," he blurted. She took it and glanced inside. With a scoff she threw the bag over her shoulder. "Was...it not good enough?"

"No roses. I'll enchant it later," she grumbled. "I know where to send you to find this man."

"Charlotte's father?"

"Were you looking for another man?" she asked, pinching the bridge of her nose.

"I'm just making sure." He didn't want to accidentally find the wrong guy. Charlotte didn't deserve that kind of disappointment.

She shook her head and went into the next room, retrieving an old-fashioned brass compass. Its needle was pointed southwest, barely a wobble even as he admired its casing. There was a fae rune etched into the base.

"I think it's broken," he said, as the needle didn't move even as he turned with the compass in his palm.

He glanced to Izell, whose face was set with a mixture of amusement and exasperation. "That's one of my finest seeker compasses, Armando. It's enchanted to find the one you've been looking for."

"It's...oh! It's pointing toward him," he said, holding the compass that much tighter. "Thank you, thank you so much. Wait. How far away is he?" He inspected the glossy face of the tool for any hint of that.

She smiled to herself. "Far, but not too far."

What an unhelpful, fae kind of answer. "Like, a day's drive? Would I burn up in the sun if I started driving now?"

She tapped her chin with a sharp fingernail before gesturing toward him. A wave of magic flowed over his skin with a wake of goosebumps. "If you want to find him, you will go now," she said, flicking her wrist in dismissal.

Instead of taking his leave, he pulled her into a hug. Most wouldn't dare, fearing the sharpness of her tongue or the sting of her magic, but he knew there was more to her than that. "I don't know what you had to do for this, but—"

Izell's eyes twinkled. "Believe it or not, I'm just the messenger."

ARMANDO PROPPED THE COMPASS ON THE DASH, USING HIS phone for leverage. He drove with the sky lightening at his back.

For a few moments, he feared what would happen if Izell's spell failed as the sun's rays caressed the back of his head. Yet nothing sizzled.

Not much changed, either, except that he'd picked up a thirty-ounce coffee from a drive-through and fought off stray yawns in the gaps between the peppy music he played. He'd crossed the state line into New Jersey some time ago and split his gaze between the road and the compass needle, hyperaware of its every twitch.

This car was Julian's second one, the type of vehicle a vampire took when they didn't want attention. Armando wasn't too impressed with it, as he caught the sound of a whine when he pushed the gas too hard or the way it shook when he hit the brakes. As he hit stop-and-go traffic in the Philadelphia area, he took a peek at the registration.

The car was twenty years old. He sighed to himself and made a mental note to tell Julian older vehicles needed more care than this one had apparently gotten.

That wasn't the end of his woes, though. Clouds clustered across the sky, soon choking the air with snow flurries. Traffic slowed to a snail's crawl. "C'mon," he grumbled, his coffee lukewarm at best as he swirled it impatiently. He shouldn't have had the impression that this would be easy when he hadn't even found the guy yet.

What would he say? "Hi, I'm Armando. Your daughter's lifemate," he said, meeting his gaze in the rearview mirror and trying to put on a friendly expression. "You didn't know you had a daughter? Well, uh, surprise!"

No, that wouldn't work.

He pep talked himself into the afternoon, only stopping for gas. Even when the compass guided him to skim Philadelphia and switch interstates to head northwest, the weather was steadily worsening. It felt like nighttime. To his light-sensitive vampire eyes, a blessing. But problematic for everyone else. Several accidents from overeager mortals returning to family meant he was worried he wouldn't find Charlotte's father and return with him in time for Christmas.

If Armando could figure out what to say to him to get him to come back to New York in the first place. He was so caught up in it that he didn't think to question the compass when it turned again...until he recognized a sign he'd passed before. "Hey, don't lead me in circles," he said, scowling at its brass face.

It didn't change its bearing until it pointed toward an exit from the interstate. "Trusting you," he muttered, glancing at the time. Four in the afternoon. Any sane vampire would be asleep by now, not braving a snowstorm during a time the sun should be up.

Maybe the compass would take him to a house. It could be ideal to do this now, when Charlotte's father wouldn't be moving around. He was still considering positive what-ifs when the car jumped forward, releasing a puff of black smoke from under the hood. Armando cursed as he felt something give way. Brakes worked, but the gas pedal didn't. He guided the vehicle to the side of the road and rested his forehead on the wheel.

Tapping against it a few times, he released a litany of curses for the old piece of junk. Julian probably hadn't changed the oil or something. It wasn't like Armando was a car guy himself, but at least his stuff had never crapped out on him to leave him in a snowbank with more flakes accumulating over the windshield.

He pocketed his phone and took up the compass. "I blame you," he told it. Though he was loath to leave the bubble of warmth in the vehicle, he wasn't about to sit around and wait for help. He'd push the car to a mechanic, but first he had to find the closest one.

Boots crunching against the snow, he drew his coat up to his chin and knitted cap all the way over his brow and ears. He followed the curve of the ramp down the rest of the way to this side street, where there was a convenience store on either corner. Bingo. He trundled his way inside the first one, grabbing a package of candy and the knowledge that a repair shop was still open a few miles down the road.

Sighing, he decided to hoof it to the shop first. He could get in line for attention, flash some cash, and try to get the car up and running by nightfall. Maybe if he was lucky, the snow would let up and he could still find Charlotte's father in time. He munched his candy on the way there, savoring the sweetness. Vampires could still eat solid food, but he didn't need it anymore. He'd always thought the super-skinny and svelte look of a vampire who only drank blood was unappealingly small, so he ate to keep up his own appearance.

He hunched over to fight against a blast of icy wind. It felt like the very elements didn't want him to succeed, like this was a trial to earn what he really wanted. He thought of Charlotte. How her smile would be accentuated with full vampire fangs. What would she think when she realized he was her lifemate all along? Would it be shock or relief to finally know why he'd never given up hope for a date?

Something vibrated in his coat pocket. His brow creased as he fished out the compass. Its needle pointed straight ahead, gleaming with its own light. As he glanced up, he saw he was on the drive of an automotive shop.

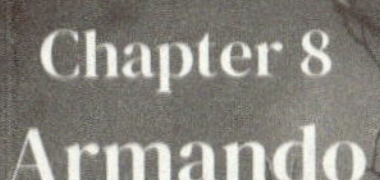

Chapter 8
Armando

The door was locked, but a teen let him in and sat behind the reception desk. "Can I help you, sir?" she asked, setting aside a cell phone as she fumbled with pens and a stack of paper. The little space was decorated with a tiny Christmas tree and miles of tinsel and string lights. Someone had been very bored, he thought.

"I need my car fixed. It broke down not far from here," he said, flashing his best smile despite how his bones ached the moment he sat down. This room abutted the shop, where he heard someone working with power tools.

She told him they had only one mechanic working right now, and a sense of surety gripped Armando as he asked, "What's his name?"

Her brow creased, as if it were an odd question. "His name is Darius."

"Yeah?" He shot to his feet. "I need to talk to him."

"Sir, that area is off—" The door slammed behind him as he entered a space made to hold several cars. A variety of power tools and equipment hung on the walls all around.

There was one vehicle in the shop at the moment, and the mechanic rolled out from underneath it to fix him with a steely look. He'd seen that face hundreds of times for every bad idea he'd ever uttered in Charlotte's presence. "No guests in the shop," the man said, sitting up when Armando didn't move. "Safety 101, sir, don't want you getting hurt."

Armando's gaze flashed from the embroidered "Darius" on the man's overalls to the vitiligo spots breaking up the brown of his skin around his neck and face. He sensed a fellow vampire as well.

"I need to talk to you," he blurted.

Darius released a weary sigh. "If you want to schedule in a vehicle, talk to the receptionist."

"No no, you don't understand. I, um..." Yeah, this was going well. So much for the hours of pep talk and going over what to say to this man. All of it had fallen out of Armando's brain with the shock of being face-to-face with the right person.

He cleared his throat. "My name is Armando Nizzola, and I came to tell you about your daughter."

Surprise colored Darius's expression. "I believe you're in the wrong place," he said carefully.

"If you're thinking, 'I don't have a daughter,' then that's okay. That's why I wanted to tell you about her," he said, feeling his palms moisten. He pulled up a picture on his phone of Charlotte smiling wide enough to show her short fangs, mid-laugh at something dumb he'd said. It was a candid moment, one of those pictures his female friends always wanted deleted.

He showed it to Darius, hoping he would see some resemblance. "Her name is Charlotte Smith, and she's a dhampir. She's been looking for you for a long time."

Grabbing a towel to wipe grease off his hands, Darius used it to hold the device closer to his face. "You try this on every vampire you meet?" he asked.

"What do you mean?"

Darius passed the phone back to him, shaking his head. "I don't have a daughter. That girl doesn't even look like me." He circled his face and neck with one hand. Scoffing, he bent to retrieve his rolling bench.

Wetting his lips, Armando pulled out the one fact he hoped Charlotte and this man had in common. "Marlene," he said.

Darius paused and shot a look over his shoulder. "What did you say?"

"Her mother's name was Marlene." He waited for a spark of recognition, anything. The other man stared at him stonily.

"Did you need a car repaired, or what?" he asked instead.

"That's not the point. I came here to find you because you're the only person in this whole world who can turn her into a vampire." A note of pleading entered his tone as Darius sat on the bench, his arms crossed. "I know this is a lot from a stranger, but hear me out. She's been looking for you for a very long time. All she's ever known about you is your first name and your skin condition. You are her gateway to a better life. An *immortal* life."

Darius inspected his knuckles and the vitiligo on his skin. "Marlene would be an old woman by now. She and I parted on bad terms, but I never expected..."

Armando bit his tongue, watching the other man as he considered. This was the hardest part, the waiting. Making sure Darius overcame the shock of learning about something and someone he'd missed for decades.

"She never got over that I was a vampire. I respected her wishes and left. Far away from her, so far she couldn't even tell me...we had a child together." Darius shook his head, his shoulders sagging. "How did you find me? How did you know you found the right guy?"

"Little bit of magic." Very few vampires knew about the real magic of fae. To say anything more would start an explanation that would take all night. "Little bit of luck, too. I'm Charlotte's lifemate, you see. We've both been trying to find you."

Darius smiled and released a disbelieving laugh. "To think anyone wants to find me. But you did. Is it Christmas yet?"

"Not yet. Would you like to meet her, though? For Christmas?" Armando offered.

"I'd love to," Darius murmured. "Just...let me finish this shift."

"Oh, um. Got room to repair another car?"

Before he knew it, he was pushing Julian's old vehicle through the snow alongside Charlotte's father, both of them in good spirits despite the cold.

THE DRIVE BACK FELT LIKE A QUIZ. THEY PLAYED TWENTY questions Charlotte Smith style, where Armando tried to answer with the depth of everything he knew about her that wasn't too personal. He felt a little guilty sharing that she'd once been a glorified servant to the leader of Coven Rosas, who'd kept her around as a bodyguard by restricting who she fed from.

Darius fumed over the knowledge. "Tell me the name of the man who did this to my little girl," he demanded.

Armando glanced over nervously. "She's out of that situation, and they're decent with each other. There's no need to pick a fight." And as far as he could tell, Darius was a rogue, otherwise known as a vampire without a coven. He'd laid low all this time to avoid being caught up in inter-coven warfare. Picking a fight with a coven master was exactly the opposite of what he should do upon getting to New York.

Darius had packed a single bag for the trip. He lived on his own, with no family left to visit for the holidays until now. "Well, fine," he grumbled.

The snowfall was slowing, making the return trip much smoother than Armando's marathon. Darius drove, with Armando running GPS on his phone to take him to New York the most efficient route. They'd left Julian's car in the shop to make it an overnight journey and give Darius the opportunity to shower and shave.

"She's going to be so happy to see you," Armando said, deflecting them back to the joy of the moment to come. No matter what followed, at least she would finally know the mysterious father that was her vampire heritage.

"Do you think she'll want to become a vampire right away?" Darius had quickly realized that was part of the urgency of searching him out.

"That's entirely up to her." But Armando hoped she would. Since she was already half-turned, surely the transition would be easy for her.

The two men lapsed into an easy silence as the New York skyline filled the horizon. The moon peeked out between the clouds, lighting the way home.

45

Chapter 9
Charlotte

Charlotte slept in. Her thumb hovered over Armando's name several times that night, wondering where he'd gone off to since, for once, he wasn't texting her casually to pass the time on an evening off.

She couldn't complain about time off, except she totally could. After the wonder of a fae festival to occupy her mind with colors and noise, her sleepy little house seemed dull by comparison. As did the sappy Christmas specials on television.

"Ugh." She shut off the television and rested her eyes, sighing. She'd already set out the dress she'd wear for the Christmas Eve party tomorrow and a variety of accessories she'd bought to go with it. She remembered last year's event, a huge party celebrating that they all were alive and had survived the insanity of demons determined to usher in the apocalypse.

Hopefully this year's bash was tamer. Less drinking, more gifts. A real Christmas event. She knew Olivia and Violet were spending time with their men, and a twinge of jealousy hit her that she wasn't wherever Armando had gone.

She bounced her knee as her mind turned over an array of ideas. She couldn't deny that she was attracted to Armando—his sense of humor, his patience with her, and not to mention that smile. Even if the djinni had looked her in the face with three eyes and said, "wish granted," there was still no vampire father figure showing up at her door. But Charlotte could admit to herself it was time.

She was ready to kiss Armando's silly face. It was past time for her to plant her lips on his and say that they could figure out the rest as they went.

In the midst of her whiling away the time, a car honked right outside her window. She shrugged it off, thinking it was one of her neighbors being obnoxious. And then someone really laid on the horn to show her the true meaning of "annoying."

She drew up the blinds, ready to give that person a piece of her mind. Instead, she saw Armando leaning out of the window of an unfamiliar car as it pulled into her drive. He waved urgently with both hands, motioning for her to come outside.

"Of course it's him," she said to herself, putting on a coat and heading out. She was careful stepping off the porch, having learned the hard way how the steps iced over moments after the first snowflake hit the ground in late autumn.

Armando met her halfway, biting his lip to keep from smiling too brightly. "Hey," he said.

"Hey. You could've, you know, texted," she said.

"My phone died," he admitted, showing her a dark screen as he pulled it from his back pocket. Now that she looked at him more closely, he seemed exhausted and jittery, as if only awake due to regular shots of coffee. But those jitters meant something else as he turned to gesture to the car.

Someone else was getting out and dusting off invisible wrinkles on a thick sweater. He wasn't someone she knew, except deep down, she did the moment he turned and their gazes met. The vitiligo was hard to miss. But she looked into eyes like his every day in the mirror. She recognized the uncertainty in the set of his lips.

Her father. Wish granted. She pulled an Olivia, releasing a breathy cry somewhere in the octaves of an excited scream. She held the nearest person, Armando, clinging as she rode a wave of emotions. "That's him," she said, waiting for the most minute of confirmations.

He nodded. "Yup! I got him."

She moved without thinking, pressing her lips to his in the midst of her delight. It was their very first kiss, and she hadn't meant any romance here. At least not yet. But she recoiled a second later from a pulse of electric shock on that contact.

Her eyes widened as she took a step back, touching her still-tingling lips. *How strange. Must be the storm,* she reasoned, turning to greet her father for the first time.

She was within a pace, her hand outstretched, when she decided to just go for a hug instead. Embracing a stranger wasn't the weirdest thing she'd done. "Are you Darius?" she asked without letting go of him.

"Yes. And you must be Charlotte," he said, grasping her shoulders to take a good look at her face. "You look just like your mother. Marlene." He spoke with a wistful sigh, brushing a curl behind one of her ears.

She nodded, feeling her eyes sting. "It's really you. You're really here." It was a moment out of any of her dreams, but there was one thing here that marked it as reality. She turned to Armando, who waited with his hands in his pockets, watching the wind caress the tiny set of chimes she'd strung up on her porch.

"You guys want to come inside?" she offered.

SHE SAT WITH DARIUS LATE INTO THE MORNING. ARMANDO had plugged in his phone to charge and hung out for an hour or so until calling Julian to pick him up so he could rest at his own place. She hated that he seemed like a third wheel, but she was glad to get some time alone with her father.

She could pinch herself. The man she'd searched so hard for, only a few states away all this time. Instead of getting caught up in vampire politics, he'd laid low and repaired cars. Cars didn't ask questions about his diet habits, and as long as he worked hard, no one seemed to care that he was oddly enthusiastic to take the night shifts at the shops he worked at.

"Armando really broke down two miles from you?" she asked in the midst of his story.

How incredible, really. She saw the djinni's work in there somewhere. Maybe it was the mysterious compass that'd pointed out the way or how the very thing her father could fix was what broke within walking distance. Going to Faerie was one of the best things she'd ever done.

"He really did. Burst into my shop and changed my life," he said. "I packed a bag, and here I am."

"Did you take it in? You're free to stay here," she offered. She was happy to lend out her guest bedroom. This house was too large for just her. Even though she'd just met Darius, she had the feeling she could trust him to share a roof for the day.

"Are you sure? I could try to find a hotel."

"No way. Not this close to Christmas," she protested.

He ended up getting his stuff to spend the day here. She only showed him the guest bedroom after a tour of the house, though, pausing before a collage of pictures. Some were new and glossy, showing her smiling with her friends or posing in front of the new house she'd bought with her own money.

"This house is the first stable place I've had that's all mine," she admitted, her thumb resting on the frame of a picture of her hugging the side of the porch with a silly smile. "I've bounced around a lot."

His gaze flashed from that picture to others above it. Faded and preserved by this point, they were images of her with other family. She'd aged normally until she was exiting her teen years. Following the progression of time were pictures of her and her mother, Marlene. While Charlotte stayed the same, Marlene started to age in each until she was a wise old woman with a cap of white curls and a gentle smile.

"I could take you to visit her if you like," she said in a hush. "She's not buried far from here."

His eyes shimmered in the low light. "I would like that."

She had another reason for showing these immortalized memories to him. They were proof. If he didn't recognize Marlene, well, he wasn't her pops. But now she felt herself getting misty too, wishing her mother was still around to see this moment.

Maybe she could find Saniya and ask for it one day. What person didn't want their mother back, though? Who wouldn't want their parents to be together and happy again?

She would hold on to what she had. A small miracle she couldn't just thank a djinni for. No, the one who'd made her wish come true was Armando, and she'd been so excited she'd barely thanked him. She vowed to change that the next time she saw him.

"Anyway, you probably want to get to bed," she said rather than bore him with extended tales of her new job and life.

"It has been an exciting day." She felt his attention on her as she took him to the guest room, which she'd decorated with abstract designs and splashes of color. It was so unlike the man she'd only begun to know that she had to laugh to see him there.

Still, he took it in and set his bag on the bed. "One more thing," he said. "Do you want some of my blood?"

Charlotte's mouth popped open in surprise. Usually, she was wary of offers of blood. Her current host was Armando, who offered with no strings attached. But most folks wanted something—even just her protection—for a taste of their blood.

With Darius, it was different. His blood matched the vampirism in her own veins. As she understood it, even one drop could make her existence as half-human unstable.

"Yes, please." She practically quivered with the anticipation of finally being a full-blooded vamp. No more dhampir jokes. No more being second-guessed. And best of all, she could finally date another immortal without fear of someday being a burden.

She held up a finger as she drew her phone out, shooting off a few quick messages. "I just need to call in a friend or two to help."

A few minutes later, the air pressure shifted around them. The doorbell rang.

Darius turned a curious look her way as she bustled over to answer the door. A portal was just closing behind them, courtesy of Violet. As the coven master's mate, she was often in close contact with the couple on her doorstep, Samuel and Melanie Rainey, the deputy and his wife. Melanie also just so happened to be the coven's resident doctor.

"You needed me urgently?" The woman gave Charlotte a quick once-over as she and Samuel stepped inside.

"Sam, Mel, meet Darius...my father." She saw the realization set in for them quickly.

Samuel rushed forward to shake Darius's hand enthusiastically and slap him on the shoulder. "Great to meet you, mate," he said. "Here for the sights, or here to stay?"

"I'm thinking of staying," he answered.

As Samuel started asking him questions for screening new members, Charlotte turned to his wife. "He offered me his blood," she said in an undertone. "I was hoping you could monitor me? If that's not too much to ask."

Melanie was usually as serious as a heart attack, so even the hint of cheer in her expression was like a shout of joy. "It would be a pleasure. I've never actually witnessed a dhampir's turning."

"Am I about to be a science experiment, doc?" she asked with a hint of nerves. She was used to being most vampires' only dhampir friend.

"Definitely not. How about we lay you down and get this started?"

Charlotte got herself changed in the bathroom into something comfortable to sleep in before gathering up her father and Melanie. He bit his wrist and offered the twin lines of blood to her. After taking the coppery drink, she barely remembered what came next. Her dreams were dark and warm, like a comforting blanket of peace.

BUT WAKING TRADED THAT PEACE FOR VERTIGO THE MOMENT she swung herself out of bed. She reached up to steady her head too quickly, slapping her forehead instead.

"Ugh!"

There was no question it'd worked. She still remembered the first time her blood activated its vampire side in her early twenties. Same deal. She would move too fast, break things like toothbrushes and doorknobs accidentally, and overwhelm her senses the moment she encountered light or noise.

Merry Christmas! She forced herself to smile through the dizzy spell of standing up. This was what she wanted. And she'd gotten used to it before.

She turned on the bathroom light with her eyes scrunched closed. Peeling them open one at a time, she murmured encouragement to herself as she glanced in the mirror.

Tiny changes made themselves known in the shape of her brow and the bow of her lips. Just the beginning of a change she felt within herself, heading straight for full-blooded vampirehood.

Would she be a fledgling? She wondered if she could skip the most dreaded part of the change, when the bloodlust was endless. Her belly felt full, and so did her mouth as she inspected the tips of her fangs. Debating whether they were longer or if that was just her, she checked the time on her phone and gasped.

It was Christmas Eve, and she would miss the party if she didn't rush.

Chapter 10
Armando

Armando bounced on the balls of his feet out in the cold, his head on a swivel as party guests filtered by. His message log with Charlotte contained far too many "hey's" and question marks from him with nothing from her. If he didn't want to seem desperate, well...

One glance at a barrage of messages like that and he probably seemed that way. He wanted to talk to her, to know how she and her dad were getting along. If maybe she'd already accepted his blood and become a vampire. But what if something had happened to her during the change?

Her car pulled up to the mansion after far too long, and his phone dinged with an incoming message. "I'm here!" the text read.

Yeah, he knew. He waited as she and Darius walked to the front door. She was in a dress under a heavy coat, showing a peek of red at the collar. Red, good. He'd put on a red tie hoping they would match. Like they'd planned it.

Darius wore a suit, looking like he was ready for an interview rather than a holiday event. If things went well, he'd join their coven and be able to move in close to know his daughter better.

"Sorry for keeping you waiting," Charlotte said, rushing forward and wobbling like she was in heels. Darius moved quickly to hold her arm before she face-planted.

"It's okay, *amica*. Is everything all right?" he asked. His gaze was on her shoes, which were sturdy and flat. When they embraced, she hugged him like a vice, far tighter than he was used to.

"Everything's great. Guess what," she breathed in his ear.

Oh, she could do that any day. His toes curled as he leaned into her. "What?"

"He gave me his blood. I'm a vampire now."

He pulled back to look her over with a gasp. With her already halfway there, the change was going to be subtle. Maybe she'd slip right into it and smile with full-length fangs soon to startle those that weren't paying attention. "That's great news," he breathed.

Did she recognize that they were lifemates? Her brown eyes twinkled merrily in reflection of the festive strings of lights over the entryway. If not, he had a surprise for her at the end of the night.

He had her on his arm as they climbed the stairs to greet their boss and coven master, Alexander Rehnquist, who'd off and on tried to get Armando to wait inside so he wouldn't freeze. Violet was tucked neatly into his side for warmth, wearing a green dress down to her ankles and a jaunty little elf hat. Alex glanced between Armando and Charlotte, flashing a hint of his crooked smile, the one that could melt a woman within a few paces.

He clapped Armando on the shoulder. "Time to come in, eh?"

"Sorry, boss..." Armando glanced to Charlotte, who'd parted from him briefly.

She was engaging in a lady ritual he was vaguely familiar with. "Cute hat," she was saying.

"I love your shoes!" Violet was saying back.

Armando dropped his voice. "Did we miss the proposal?" He hoped, apparently in vain, that the women would miss this particular exchange.

Both of them burrowed unerring attention into him. "What proposal?" Charlotte asked.

"Business proposal, very boring, very dry," Alex said quickly.

"Besides, you came in with this man behind you. Who would you happen to be, good sir?" He addressed Darius.

"Oh, this is my father." Charlotte jumped to make introductions. Darius seemed nervous as he greeted Alex for the first time.

"Family on a day like today. Joyous news. Why don't you go inside? The feast should be starting any minute," Alex suggested, giving Armando a pointed look and a jerk of his head.

He figured that meant the proposal hadn't happened yet. Alex shooed Violet off too, meaning he had two suspicious women flanking him as they headed inside. Their host had dragged out all the furniture to make banquet seating both inside and out. The highest-ranking members sat inside—and for once, he was glad to be Head Enforcer, because that meant he had a place at those tables with Charlotte.

"So, are you going to tell us?" Violet turned hopeful, shiny eyes his way.

He cleared his throat, searching for any distraction. It wafted past his nose as the first course of the feast was being laid out. It was one time of year every vampire in the coven ate solid food. Without the coven master and his deputy seated, Alex must've given the cue for it to start without them. "Doesn't that smell good?" he said instead, hurrying to the table to sit. His name was on a card reserving two seats, while Violet split off to sit beside the head of the table.

They were amongst coven leadership, all important men and woman and some of Alex's close friends. Julian and Olivia were breaking bread alongside Violet, while other familiar faces toasted one another.

His uncle glanced over and lifted a hand in greeting. He definitely seemed nervous, but it wasn't time yet. The first course came and went with Charlotte giving him the side eye as he remained mum about his slip-up.

Alex and Samuel joined them at the head of the table as Darius sat across from Charlotte in one of the only free spaces around. "How'd it go?" she asked.

He was beaming. "You must have a good reputation around here."

"You're in?" She clasped her hands, waiting on bated breath.

"Yes! I'm going to look for jobs in the area after the holidays."

Armando didn't mention that joining the coven wasn't particularly hard. He knew his boss had a soft spot for his community of former rogues and outcasts. Instead, he toasted when they did. "To your new start," he said.

"I'll drink to that." The other man laughed.

And so they did into the late hours of the night. Food was set aside for good wine, and the gifts came out.

Charlotte produced a slim wooden box tied with a bow. "I got you this from Faerie," she explained as he opened it and pulled out...a wooden bread knife? He glanced to her in puzzlement. "Apparently, it is the perfect whittling knife despite the shape. Magic."

"Magic," he agreed, marveling at the perfect grain in the blade and handle. It looked like it was carved from one piece of wood. Frankly, he wouldn't think to use it to whittle when it seemed like it'd break the moment any pressure was put on it. But because the m-word, magic, was being tossed in with it, he'd give it a try.

"I got you your dad?" It came out as a question despite himself. He was terrible with gifts, but when Charlotte and Darius exchanged a glance, he knew this one was perfectly welcome.

"Thanks again," she said, lacing her hand in his. She wasn't miffed at his secret anymore, instead sharing the sweet expression he loved to see curling her lips. "Words really can't capture my gratitude."

"Seeing you happy is its own reward," he murmured, wanting to kiss her then and there. Maybe at the end of the night, when there were fewer eyes on them.

Then again, most everyone was occupied by their gift-giving. Alex had opened a similar wooden box and was inspecting a vial of liquid as short and thin as his pinky. Violet whispered in his ear, and he gestured to her. She shook her head, motioning back to him. He covered his heart dramatically, whispering something that had her laughing. They shared a kiss of their own, the kind that didn't mind that others were watching.

Charlotte's gaze jumped to Julian, who'd nearly knocked his chair over as he stood. "Oh, he put on the glove," she remarked.

An old-fashioned leather piece, he noted, which glowed and molded to the shape of his hand as he stared at it. The whole party was staring too as a *pop* sounded. His fine suit was replaced in a blink by a full suit of armor. "Wow, cool." He sounded years younger as he looked down at himself.

"So *that's* what the guy meant," Olivia announced, admiring him from her seat.

Julian took a glance around. "Well, now that I have everyone's attention...do you think my clothes will come back if I take it off?" he asked.

"Take it off!" called Samuel, grinning from ear to ear.

As he took off the gauntlet, Armando hoped his uncle wasn't about to pop into a birthday suit or something. Now that would change the party atmosphere in a hurry. Luckily, the armor left like it'd never been molded to his form, and his suit was back. He offered Olivia a hand up.

Armando nudged Charlotte urgently. She wasn't the only one who gasped when Julian went down on one knee and presented a ring to his lifemate. A feminine sigh preceded polite applause as Olivia fanned herself and nodded, too choked up to say yes except for a squeak of noise.

He turned to Charlotte, admiring the glimmer in her eyes. *Just wait,* he thought. *That could be us in a year.*

"Okay, that was worth the secret," she admitted, flashing him a smile.

"He's been a mess for days," Armando confided. "I'm shocked Olivia didn't notice."

Charlotte whispered behind a hand. "Actually, she thought he was developing an anxiety disorder." They shared a laugh at that.

He leaned back in his chair, pondering over when best to break his news to Charlotte. The party was winding down around them with that burst of excitement. At any point, he could just reach over and press his lips to hers. It was possible her transformation was enough along that she'd recognize the sparks and butterflies feeling of kissing a lifemate.

A ball of mistletoe was wiggled over them. "Kiss, kiss!" a drunk partygoer giggled, holding a stick with the mistletoe hanging by a string.

He didn't need more encouragement than that. Turning to Charlotte, he drew her closer for a brush of their lips. No static this time, just warmth lingering in his chest when they parted after a long moment.

She pressed her fingers to her lips, realization setting in as she gasped again. "Armando, um…"

"Yes?" He couldn't help a grin. He'd been waiting for this moment for so long.

Her hands cupped her mouth. "Are we lifemates?" she asked in a shocked whisper.

"It's about time you noticed." He winked, laughing when she cried out and wrapped her arms around him.

And there were tears. He smoothed his hand down her back, puzzled by the twin trails rolling down her face. "Why didn't you tell me?" she asked, blotting at her eyes with a napkin.

"I wanted it to be a surprise. Are you surprised?" He offered his most winning smile.

"Am I…?" She leaned away from him, fanning her face. "This is the best day of my life. You really waited for me for a whole year?"

And he would've waited longer if he had to. His chest felt full that she finally knew because she'd found out the right way. "I sure did. And now I have a question for you."

She gave him an expectant look as he drew out the moment. "Will you be my girlfriend?" he asked, clasping his hands.

Charlotte giggled and kissed him again, her answer in the way her lips lingered. But in case of any doubt, she breathed a yes just between the two of them.

"We're getting better at that," she said, resting her head on his shoulder. "Merry Christmas, Armando."

Dhampir's Wish

"Merry Christmas, *ragazza*. To many more."
"Many, many more," she agreed.

Also by Elise Hennessy
Altare World

Are you ready for a high-flying adventure on gryphon-back? Join Sivana as she becomes the first female cadet at the highly competitive Gryphon Rider Academy after the blind gryphon Arimus chooses her as his new rider.

Dragon Riders of Pern meets Song of the Lioness in this YA fantasy series in which a pair of underdogs rewrite what's possible in a formerly all-boys military academy.

- See Gryphon Rider Academy on Amazon -

Join an unlikely crew of five misfits and a mouse as they strive to become one of Altare's newest elite spy teams. Heists and adventures await!

The Gilded Wolves meets Six of Crows in this YA fantasy series in which a former thief uses her skills to become a spy. If you like clever heroines, strong friendships, and found family, then you'll love Royal Spy Institute!

- See Royal Spy Institute on Amazon -

About the Author

Elise Hennessy is an author of young adult fantasy full of adventure and found family. She holds a master's degree in journalism and enjoys crafting unique stories. When Elise is not busy writing, she's trying to reduce her prodigious TBR list. She lives in Texas with her family and is owned by two cats.

Find out more about her books at: www.elisehennessy.com